For the real boss,
Sam Hest

A. H.

For Sophie
and the new baby

J. B.

Text copyright © 1997 by Amy Hest
Illustrations copyright © 1997 by Jill Barton

First edition 1997

Library of Congress Cataloging-in-Publication Data

Hest, Amy.
You're the boss, Baby Duck / Amy Hest ; illustrated by
Jill Barton. — 1st U.S. ed.
Summary: When her parents make such a fuss over
their new baby, Baby Duck feels neglected, until Grampa
helps her to realize that she is still important.
ISBN 1-56402-667-1
[1. Ducks — Fiction. 2. Babies — Fiction. 3. Grandfathers — Fiction.]
I. Barton, Jill, ill.   II. Title.
PZ7.H4375Yo   1997
[E] — dc21   96-46640

2 4 6 8 10 9 7 5 3 1

Printed in Italy

This book was typeset in Opti Lucius Ad Bold.
The pictures were done in pencil and watercolor.

Candlewick Press
2067 Massachusetts Avenue
Cambridge, Massachusetts 02140

You're the Boss, Baby Duck!

Amy Hest

illustrated by Jill Barton

CANDLEWICK PRESS
CAMBRIDGE, MASSACHUSETTS

Baby Duck was having a bad day.
There was a brand-new baby in the house,
and everyone was making a great big fuss
for no good reason.

"What a fine little face," cooed Mrs. Duck.

"Don't you love her little beak?"

"No," Baby said.

"What fine little feet," trilled Mr. Duck.

"Isn't she hot stuff?"

"No," Baby said.

Baby Duck sat by herself. She sang a little song.

"*Send that no-good Hot Stuff back,*
No one wants her here.
Her beak is fat, her feet are fat,
And I'm the only baby."

"Are you singing to your baby sister?"
called Mr. Duck. "What a fine sister you are!"
Baby stopped singing.

Baby got up and hopped on
one foot. "Look at me!"

Mrs. Duck kissed Hot Stuff on her
fat little beak. She forgot to look.

Baby rolled over.

"Look at me!"

Mr. Duck tickled Hot Stuff on her
fat little feet. He forgot to look.

Baby Duck turned
pages in her book.
"I can read,"
she said.

Mrs. Duck put Hot Stuff into Baby's old coat.

Mr. Duck tucked
Hot Stuff into
Baby's old
carriage.

They did not hear her read.

"Time to show Grampa your brand-new baby sister!" called Mr. and Mrs. Duck.

Baby Duck stomped along. She dragged her feet and mumbled.

"That bad baby is in my carriage,
Wearing my nice coat.
I hope she goes away today
And stays away forever."

Grampa was waiting at the kitchen door.

He looked in the carriage.

"Welcome," he said.

Then he kissed Baby's cheeks.

"Bad day?" he asked.

"Yes," Baby said.

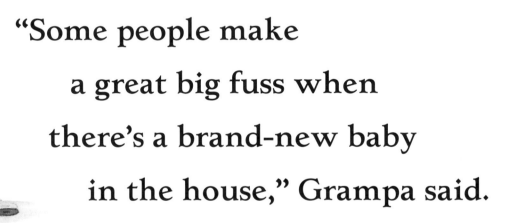

"Some people make
a great big fuss when
there's a brand-new baby
in the house," Grampa said.

"Yes," Baby said.

"I am making lunch," Grampa
said. "Want to help?"

"Yes," Baby said.

Baby Duck and Grampa made lemonade.

Grampa squeezed lemons.

Baby poured sugar.

"You are a good helper," Grampa said.

"Brand-new babies are bad helpers,"
Baby said.

"Oh, yes," Grampa said. "Brand-new babies
don't do much. They don't know how."

Baby Duck and Grampa made sandwiches
with jam. Baby got the bread. Grampa
got some jam.

"Not that jam," Baby said. "*That* one."

"You're the boss, Baby Duck," Grampa said.

"Yes," Baby said. "I am!"

The sandwiches were a big hit.

And of course the lemonade.

After lunch Baby put Hot Stuff
in her wagon.

"No crying," Baby said. "I'm the boss."

Hot Stuff did not cry.

"Look at me!"

Baby hopped on one foot.

Hot Stuff looked.

She gurgled.

"Look at me!" Baby rolled over.

Hot Stuff looked.

She burbled.

"Now I will read you a story."
Baby turned pages
in her book.

Hot Stuff gurgled. She giggled and
burbled and babbled.

After that, Baby Duck pulled Hot Stuff all around the yard. She sang a little song.

"Brand-new babies are a pain,
Fuss, fuss, fuss, fuss, fuss.
Maybe you can stay two days,
But Baby Duck is boss!"